Dear Parents:

Congratulations! Your child is taking the first steps on an exciting journey. The destination? Independent reading!

STEP INTO READING® will help your child get there. The program offers five steps to reading success. Each step includes fun stories and colorful art or photographs. In addition to original fiction and books with favorite characters, there are Step into Reading Non-Fiction Readers, Phonics Readers and Boxed Sets, Sticker Readers, and Comic Readers—a complete literacy program with something to interest every child.

Learning to Read, Step by Step!

Ready to Read Preschool–Kindergarten
• big type and easy words • rhyme and rhythm • picture clues
For children who know the alphabet and are eager to begin reading.

Reading with Help Preschool–Grade 1
• basic vocabulary • short sentences • simple stories
For children who recognize familiar words and sound out new words with help.

Reading on Your Own Grades 1–3
• engaging characters • easy-to-follow plots • popular topics
For children who are ready to read on their own.

Reading Paragraphs Grades 2–3
• challenging vocabulary • short paragraphs • exciting stories
For newly independent readers who read simple sentences with confidence.

Ready for Chapters Grades 2–4
• chapters • longer paragraphs • full-color art
For children who want to take the plunge into chapter books but still like colorful pictures.

STEP INTO READING® is designed to give every child a successful reading experience. The grade levels are only guides; children will progress through the steps at their own speed, developing confidence in their reading. The F&P Text Level on the back cover serves as another tool to help you choose the right book for your child.

Remember, a lifetime love of reading starts with a single step!

TM & copyright © by Dr. Seuss Enterprises, L.P. 2017

All rights reserved. Published in the United States by Random House Children's Books, a division of Penguin Random House LLC, New York. Featuring characters from *How the Grinch Stole Christmas!* by Dr. Seuss, TM & copyright © by Dr. Seuss Enterprises, L.P. 1957, renewed 1985.

Step into Reading, Random House, and the Random House colophon are registered trademarks of Penguin Random House LLC.

Visit us on the Web!
Seussville.com
StepIntoReading.com
randomhousekids.com

Educators and librarians, for a variety of teaching tools, visit us at RHTeachersLibrarians.com

Library of Congress Cataloging-in-Publication Data
Names: Rabe, Tish, author. | Brannon, Tom, illustrator.
Title: Cooking with the Grinch / by Tish Rabe ; illustrations by Tom Brannon.
Description: First edition. | New York : Random House, [2017] | Series: Step into reading.
Step 1 | Summary: The Grinch and Cindy Lou Who bake a Christmas surprise.
Identifiers: LCCN 2016034550 | ISBN 978-1-5247-1462-8 (trade pbk.) |
ISBN 978-1-5247-1463-5 (lib. bdg.)
Subjects: | CYAC: Stories in rhyme. | Baking—Fiction. | Christmas—Fiction.
Classification: LCC PZ8.3.R1145 Co 2017 | DDC [E]—dc23

Printed in the United States of America

10 9 8 7 6 5 4 3 2 1

This book has been officially leveled by using the F&P Text Level Gradient™ Leveling System.

by Tish Rabe
illustrated by Tom Brannon

Random House 🏠 New York

The Grinch goes down.

Down to the town.

He hears the bells.
Ding! Dong!
Dong! Ding!

He hears the *Whos*.

They sing!

Sing! Sing!

9

He taps a door.

It's Cindy-Lou!

She likes to cook.

The Grinch does too.

He likes to mix.

She likes to stir.

She cooks with him.

He cooks with her.

16

17

They make some treats
and start to bake.
Who will eat the
treats they make?

Max! Oh no!
No, no, no, NO!

Max! You have to
go, go, GO!

The treats are done.
Don't let them tip!

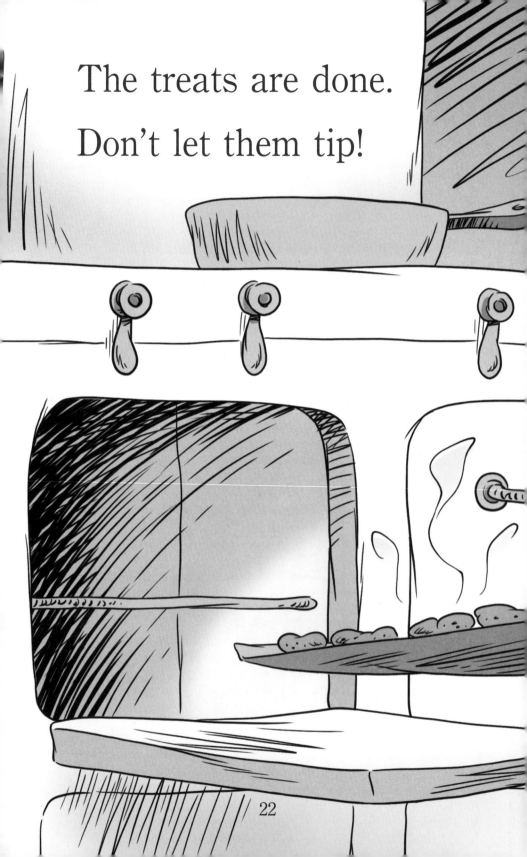

Oh no! The treats!
They start to slip!

25

Cindy-Lou is fast!

The treats do not fall.

She saves the treats.

She saves them all.

Merry Christmas, Max!
Yum, yum, yum,
yummy!

The treats are now . . .

. . . in Max's tummy!